Joseph Trudo

Swan Song

Balboa Press
A Division of Hay House
1663 Liberty Drive
Bloomington, IN 47403
www.balboapress.com
844-682-1282

Interior Image Credit: Ghada S. Timani.

ISBN: 978-1-9822-6282-2 (sc)
978-1-9822-6283-9 (e)

Library of Congress Control Number: 2021901686

Balboa Press rev. date: 01/29/2021

BALBOA.PRESS

Swan Song

*I*t was the middle of May and snow still covered much of the tundra on Alaska's north slope. A great wind blew from the Beaufort Sea pushing before it quantities of slushy snow and half frozen ice. Into this harshness there suddenly appeared a flock of swans, their long necks stretched gracefully before them, their pure white feathers blending into the whiteness of the snow around them. Two of the birds detached themselves from the flock and glided gracefully to a landing near the shore of a frozen pond. The Cob (male swans are called Cobs) and the Pen (females are called Pens) had finally arrived at their nesting ground. This particular Cob was named Albert and the Pen was called Emily. They had come to this frozen, isolated place to build a nest and raise a family. They had left their wintering ground on the east coast of the United States in late March and it had taken them almost two months to fly the long, long way to the northern shore of Alaska. They had stopped along the way, of course, to rest and eat, but it was still a very long flight and they were very glad to have finally arrived. No one knows why swans come such a long way to nest and raise a family. It had been that way for as long as swans could remember.

Albert and Emily were snug in their feather coats. Tundra swans are covered in warm, white feathers, as many as 25,000, which protect them against the fierce wind and snow. With their long journey finally finished, they just wanted to rest. They settled beside one another, folded their long necks along their backs, tucked their bills under their wings and took a well-deserved snooze. When they awoke, they immediately set to work preening, which is what swans do to clean and oil their feathers. As water birds, it was very important that their coats be dry and waterproof. Afterward, they took a short flight to look for a nesting site. It was important to have exactly the right spot for a nest. It needed to be as close to the water as possible but not too close or the nest would flood when the ice and snow melted. A little spot of dry ground surrounded by water was just right and with a bit of looking they soon found the perfect place. It was located on one end of a large pond, still partially frozen. It was a very small rise of ground located at the end of a small spit of land connecting the site with the north edge of the pond. When the ice melted, the water would rise and cover the connecting spit of land, surrounding the nest site completely by water.

Once Albert and Emily agreed upon the exact spot, they quickly set to work pulling up almost all the vegetation within 10 feet from the center of the nest. The material-grasses, sedges, lichens, moss and forbs—was replanted at the nest site and woven into a large, circular pattern. When the nest was finished, Albert and Emily stood side by side, looked at it with pride and thought "This is good". It was a fine nest, built with care and love, for it would hold their hopes for the future.

It had taken several days to build the nest and Albert and Emily were greatly helped by the hours of constant sunlight. It was early June and this far north, the sun would not set again for three months. All that light caused the lingering ice and snow to disappear quickly and the vegetation grew so fast it soon surrounded the nest with a protective shield of green to hide them from most dangers. Emily spent another day making some tiny adjustments to the nest before deciding that it was just right. Then she placed in the bottom of the nest three perfect creamy white eggs. They were large eggs, elliptical in shape and weighed almost half a pound each. Emily then entered the nest and very carefully settled herself upon the precious eggs, keeping them warm and protected from the weather and the outside world. It would take 31 days of careful incubation before the eggs hatched. In all that time, either Albert or Emily would be there to warm them, protect them and gently turn them from time to time with their bills. The long hours of constant daylight caused the vegetation to grow like crazy and the swans had a rich assortment of grasses, sedges, roots and tubers to choose from. Pondweed was a favorite of both swans as well as tasty goose tongue, pendant grass and crowfoot.. As the summer went on, nostoc algae grew everywhere and water bugs and other insects provided nutritious protein. Albert and Emily lived in a beautiful, bountiful garden and they could eat to their heart's content. Life was good.

Near the end of the first week of July, Emily was tending the nest when she felt something move. "Albert-come! Look! The eggs are hatching!" Oh, it was so exciting! After their month-long vigil, the cygnets were arriving! Over the next several hours, all three eggs hatched, and three fuzzy gray cygnets stared up from the nest at their parents. Emily greeted each of them with a low "kuk-kuk" sound as they entered the world. The first thing each cygnet saw and heard was the loving welcome of their mother's voice and their reflection in her soft brown eyes. Baby swans are called cygnets.

Since all newborn things deserve a name, Emily decided to call her new cygnets Cynthia, Samantha and Sam. Albert and Emily looked down at their three new hatchlings with great pride and the three little cygnets stared back at the wonders of the big new world they had entered. Finally, one of them spoke. "I'm hungry. When can we eat?" It was Sam and Albert beamed with pride. "That's my boy." Said Albert. "It's time for lunch." With that, Albert and Emily escorted the three little cygnets up and over the steep side of the nest and to the water's edge. "Just walk right in" said Emily, "You will float". And as easily as that, the three young cygnets were bobbing on top of the water beside their parents.

For the first two weeks of a cygnet's life, they are naturally buoyant and have no ability to "tip up" and go beneath the surface of the water. They are thus limited to "dabbling" or eating from the surface of the water. Their parents are kept busy pulling up and dragging to the surface quantities of underwater delicacies which the young then eat from the surface. Later, as they gain weight and experience, the growing cygnets are able to duck under the water and pull up their own food, but for the first two weeks their parents are kept quite busy scratching up food for the hungry young birds. When everyone in the family had eaten as much as they wanted, Albert and Emily escorted the young brood back to the nest. With full stomachs all around, Albert and Emily decided that this was a good time to begin teaching the young cygnets some of the many things they would need to know in life. One of the most important of these things was the proper way to preen. The young cygnets listened and watched closely as Emily demonstrated the proper technique. Then each of them practiced what they had learned. When they had all finished, Emily said "Good—very good. It is very, very important that you preen often and well. It will keep your feathers clean and well oiled, protecting you from the wet and cold."

When Emily had finished with the lesson on preening, Albert came forward to present his lesson. "Now kids, I don't want to scare you, but you need to know about certain dangers that can bring you great harm. I'm speaking about other creatures that want to eat you." Three young mouths flew open and three pair of young eyes got very big. Samantha began to tremble, and Cynthia edged a step closer to her mother. Sam just looked puzzled.

"What! Eat us! That's crazy talk! Why would anyone want to do that?" Sam finally said.

"Because many creatures in this world do not eat as we do. Many of them eat other creatures and a young cygnet would be a tasty snack for them."

The young birds seemed to be having trouble imagining such a terrible idea, so Albert pressed on with his explanation.

"There is danger both by land and in the air but especially in the air. Certain birds called raptors eat only flesh from other creatures. Owls, jaegers, eagles, hawks and falcons are always hunting for creatures they can carry off. Even some gulls would prove treacherous. Keep your eyes moving all the time so you see them before they see you. You never know when they might appear. The tall grass growing from the water offers a good hiding place. Stay close to your mom and me and do exactly what we tell you to do and you'll be ok. These predators cannot carry off a full-grown swan but a young cygnet is just what they're looking for to feed their young."

The youngsters thought about what their father had just told them.

"I don't feel good" said Samantha.

"My stomach hurts" said Cynthia.

"Now there's no need to be scared. It's all part of Nature's way. If you just stay close to me and your mom, you'll be OK. We know what to do to keep you safe."

"Yeah" said Sam. "Just let 'em try. You and mom will hold 'em off."

"Now I want you to listen carefully while I tell you about the dangers from the ground. These can take many forms such as bears, wolves, wolverines, foxes and short tailed weasels. Most of these can be avoided by staying well out in the pond, away from the shore."

"But the best bugs and the tastiest grass are near shore" said Sam.

"Yes, well all the bugs in the world won't help you if you get jumped by a wolf. And bears...well, bears are bad news. They're always hungry and they eat everything. They can also swim quite well. If a bear happens by, you kids stick with your mom and I'll try to lead him away before taking to the air. You can't scare bears, but you can often lead them away by making them think you're injured. Then, when you're far enough off, you can fly away. Bears can't fly." Said Albert, abruptly concluding the lesson.

"I think that's enough for today." said Emily. "Who would like some tasty Crowfoot and Goosetongue?"

"Yeah" said Sam. "Time to eat."

And with that, the pattern was set for the days to come. The swan family would feed, then return to the nest for lessons about life, followed by a short nap. Then it was back in the water to feed again. After the first day's lesson about predators and danger, the young cygnets stuck really close to Emily when she led them back into the water. In the days that followed, there was so much to learn and do that they gradually began to allow more and more distance between themselves and their parents and needed to be reminded to stay close.

One morning, about a week after the hatch, the cygnets woke up to a startling sight. "Mom! Where did all these feathers come from?" shouted Sam.

The cygnets looked around and there in the nest were several very large, white flight feathers. The feathers were far too large to have come from the cygnets and they looked toward their mother for an explanation.

"Well, children, it looks like I have begun the molt."

"Molt? What's a molt?"

"Every year, sometime in July, adult swans begin to lose their feathers. Well, not all their feathers, just the large primary flight feathers. It's nature's way of preparing us to receive new ones. So, you see, molting is a good thing because we receive strong new feathers. It takes about 33-34 days for the new feathers to grow fully. The bad part is that during that time, we cannot fly, so we must be extra alert and careful about dangers."

"Will dad lose his feathers too?" asked Cynthia.

"All adult swans go through the molt, but the cobs begin theirs about a week after the pens. When your father and I are both flightless, waiting for our new feathers to grow in, we must be especially alert and cautious because we cannot fly away from danger."

The young cygnets remembered what their father had said about bears, about how fast they could run and how well they could swim and how the only real chance for escape was to fly away. If a bear attack came during the molt, when the adults couldn't fly.... well, things could be very serious indeed. But the days went on without any bear attacks though one afternoon Emily did see a hawk in the distance and herded the cygnets into the tall grass near the pond's edge for safety, "Just in case". The remote threat passed quickly, and they all returned to feeding on the rich growths around the pond. There was no darkness at night, so the grasses and other delicious things grew quickly, and the swan family spent many hours each day eating, grooming and resting. Life was good.

One afternoon when the cygnets were about two weeks old, they discovered that they could "tip up" and put their heads under water. A whole new world suddenly opened to them and they found they were no longer dependent upon their parents to bring up food from below the pond's surface. Of course, the cygnets were still quite small birds (though they were growing amazingly fast!) and their necks weren't long enough yet to reach the pond bottom except near the shoreline where the water was not so deep. When fully grown, an adult swan can reach up to three feet under water, thanks to their long neck, but the young cygnets could only go down a few inches. Still, the ability to tip up opened whole new worlds of feeding opportunity to the young birds. One day Sam had wandered away and was feeding by himself near the shoreline enjoying life with his head underwater as he gathered a feast of water bugs and tender young shoots. As his head popped to the surface for a breath of air, he found himself face to face with a terrifying sight. There, hidden by the grass at the water's edge, was an arctic fox. The fox had laid there, perfectly still, watching Sam work his way closer and closer to the water's edge. The fox's eyes were completely fixed on the plump young cygnet, his muscles tense and ready to pounce. The fox's mouth was slightly open, and Sam could see the very sharp teeth which lined it, top and bottom.

"Awwww!...Dad, help!" his young voice called shrilly, all the while working frantically to turn himself around and head for deeper water. Then, a split second before the fox meant to leap upon the hapless young cygnet, an amazing sight occurred.

Out of the cattails and water grass 20 feet away appeared Albert, but this was not an Albert that his children had seen before. This was an angry, fearless Albert, headed directly for the threat to his young chick. His neck was fully extended, pointed directly at the fox. His wings were raised and quivering and his charge across the water came amazingly fast. He was literally running across the top of the water, rapidly closing the distance between himself and the fox, hissing fiercely all the while. An adult male tundra swan weighs about 20 pounds and has a large, impressive wingspan. Albert bore down on the fox in a furious rage, wings quivering, gaining speed with each wild step. Before the fox could refocus his attention, Albert struck him square in the side, his great wings flapping wildly and his beak striking at the fox's head. Brave Albert! Valiant Cob! The fox was knocked off his feet and could think of only one thing-escape! With the valiant cob in hot pursuit, the fox dashed wildly through the tall grass surrounding the pond and out on to the tundra. An angry Albert continued to pursue the terrified fox, hissing wildly. Finally, Albert discontinued the chase and allowed the fox to disappear in the distance. When he returned to the pond, the little family gathered close together to talk about the happening.

"Wow! Did you see Pop go? He was fierce! I thought I was a goner." Said Sam. "Rock 'em, Sock 'em, Bop 'em! You go, Pops!"

"Now, son, you wandered too close to the shore. You almost were a goner. Don't stray away from the family like that. There's safety in staying together. Don't do that again." Albert meant to scold the young cygnet more severely, but the truth was that he was so relieved and thankful for the way things had worked out that he didn't have the heart for any harshness. Still, the young chicks now had firsthand proof of how suddenly terrible things could happen and it would be a long while before the memory dimmed in their minds.

"You know" said Emily "this might be a good time to introduce the children to a lesson in physical interactions and display."

"Hmmm, I think you're right" replied Albert. "OK kids, this is important. Pay close attention. Your mom will describe some important behavior techniques and I'll display the appropriate actions."

For the remainder of the afternoon, Albert and Emily showed the chicks the various actions and techniques that swans use to communicate with both swans and other creatures. Emily described and Albert demonstrated the various postures for the Dropped Wing display, Raised Wing display, Quivering Wing Display, the Ground Stare, Foot Slapping and Forward Calls as well as the Wing Flap, Greeting Display and Submissive Posture. Albert showed them how a loud, evil hiss could be used together with a quivering wing display to sometimes startle or frighten an intruder. The cygnets loved the lesson and spent the remainder of the day practicing what they were taught. By late afternoon, they were all ready for a rest.

"It's been a good day" said Emily.

"Yes, it has." Agreed Albert. The kids have had an exciting day and learned a lot. At least I know it was an exciting day for me." He said in a low voice that only Emily could hear. Emily swam up to him gently, looked at him with her soft brown velvet eyes and whispered, "thank you".

The cygnets were growing by leaps and bounds, getting bigger each day. Their newborn plumage of gray fuzzy pinfeathers was now replaced by regular feathers of dark gray and blue. One day, Cynthia asked her mother, "When will I get beautiful white feathers, like you?"

"Oh, that will happen in due course, little one. When I was your age, I remember how anxious I was to grow up fast and have beautiful white plumage. Trust me, it will come when nature is ready for you to have it."

"But when will that be?"

"Well, it can be different for each bird, but over the winter, you will begin to molt and by next spring you will have a beautiful new coat of white to begin the migration."

"Oh, that seems so long" said Cynthia.

"You know, I do believe that this afternoon would be a good time to teach you about swan history and customs. There is much you should know about family history and traditions."

So, that afternoon during class time, Emily and Albert taught their young brood about the fascinating history of swans.

"First" said Emily, you should know that there are different families of swans. We are Tundra Swans. In past times, we were often called Whistling Swans though scientists call us by our official family name, Cygnus columbianus. Besides our family, there are our cousins, the Trumpeter swans and several close relations such as Berwick's Swan and the Whooper Swan and the Mute Swan. Different swan families live in different parts of the world but in North America there are only two main families, the Trumpeter swans and the Tundra swans. Your cousins, the Trumpeter swans, are a bit bigger and have curved necks but as you can see, our necks are straight. In Australia, there is even a Swan that is completely black."

"Ooh-cool!" said Sam.

Emily continued. "Swans have always been considered a royal, elegant, stately bird. In England, in times past, they were the exclusive property of the King. Only he could own a swan, and no one could harm them. They were one of the symbols of royalty. Swans are long lived birds whose lifespan can be 20 years or more" All of the cygnets paid close attention to their mother's lesson, but Cynthia focused especially hard upon what was being taught. "Royal... Elegant...Stately, yes, that is the desire of my heart."

"The key to proper swan behavior is serenity." their mother concluded. "Be slow and deliberate in all that you do, and the rest will follow naturally." Then and there, Cynthia determined that she would practice the virtue of serenity every day. Her behavior would always reflect honor upon both her swan family and her personal family. Using her mother as a guide, she would become the most perfectly serene swan in the whole world.

As Emily finished her lesson, Albert swam up and faced the cygnets. "Now, there are a couple more things that should be mentioned about swan behavior, history and customs": he said. "First, swans are brave, both cobs and pens. When danger threatens, we always face it head on unless the situation is totally hopeless. Other waterbirds, like ducks, will dive underwater to escape danger, but swans meet a threat face to face. We fight for our family and our territory. We don't always flee from danger, like many other birds. Of course, in desperate times, we may be forced to take to the air but by and large, we confront our dangers head on."

"The other topic I want to mention is loyalty. Swans mate for life and stay with each other through thick and thin. They both share in the duties of raising a family. Once a mate is selected, they remain loyal for the rest of their lives."

"Oh, how romantic" said Samantha. "Mom, how old were you when you met dad?"

"Oh, we were each about 2 or 3 years old when we first noticed each other, though it was another year or two before we decided to raise a family. We were five when we raised our first brood of cygnets."

"What made you choose dad from all the other cobs?" asked Samantha. "Was he bigger or stronger or more handsome?

"Well, there was just something about him that seemed very special and after a while I knew that he was the perfect cob for me. I watched him and compared him to the other cobs for quite a while before I decided that he was the one. And girls, in the swan world, it's the pen who does the choosing." Said Emily with quiet satisfaction.

"That's right" said Albert. "Your mother had plenty of other cobs who were interested in her... but, and he raised his head slightly "she chose the best."

Albert moved closer beside Emily and the two looked at each other with obvious affection.

"We've been through some interesting times together, haven't we?" said Albert.

"Indeed, we have," replied Emily, "indeed we have."

"Mom" said Samantha "you and dad talk about "Nature" a lot. Just exactly what is Nature?"

"Well, there are different ways of answering that question, but I think that the simplest way is probably the best. Nature means the natural world around us and how we fit into the rest of creation. It's how all things fit together and work for the common good."

"So, Nature is a good thing?"

"Well, at times it may seem quite harsh, but the result is a good thing. This is a very important subject, and we need to talk more about it, but right now we've had a very long and exciting day and it's time to eat."

"I hear that!" said Sam. "I can go for some tasty pondweed and juicy water bugs. Let's go!" As Emily lead the three cygnets toward a patch of pondweed, Cynthia tried her best to look serene and regal while Sam paddled eagerly ahead of the group.

The long summer days folded into one another with no change in the daily routine: Preen, eat, school, rest—then do it all over again. Under this routine, the cygnets grew rapidly. They had hatched in early July and by mid-August they had grown remarkably. Their feathers were fledging rapidly (fledging is the process of growing feathers) though it would be mid-September before they were fully fledged and ready for flight. Their fuzzy gray pinfeathers had been replaced by the dark colored real feathers of a first-year cygnet. Albert and Emily had undergone the molt in mid-July and now their strong new flight feathers had almost completely grown back. Another week would see them fully fledged: Everything seemed to be right on schedule. Life was good. Then one day in late August, a scary thing happened.

It was early afternoon, and the young family was resting after a morning of eating and swan school. The day was overcast, and it had been raining earlier. The clouds were low with patches of fog. Suddenly there was a strange sound, at first very faint but then growing louder and louder. Then, as the sound grew closer, the swans began to feel the vibration through the ground.

"What's happening?" Sam yelled but the end of his question was drowned out by the terrible noise of the thing approaching them. It was like nothing the chicks had ever experienced. Then, in an instant, the thing was over them. It circled slowly around the pond, then came to a stop in midair facing them. The noise was incredible and the wind from its wings bent the tall grass over and whipped the surface of the pond into waves. True to their swan nature, both Albert and Emily faced toward the terrible threat, but the swan chicks trembled and cowered behind their parents, no match for the great wind and horrible noise. And the smell! The clean, pure air was filled with a heavy, sickening odor. Inside the strange thing, the swans could see beings. Had the terrible thing eaten them? Was it going to eat the swan family too? Suddenly, a small space opened in the side of the thing and one of the beings inside held out a small box. There was a flash of light, and the box disappeared. Then the great thing slowly turned in midair, lowered its nose and flew away.

When it had gone, the little family sat, stunned, for a few moments. Even after it had gone, the air smelled heavily from the creature's breath. The silence was finally broken by Sam. "What was that!" he asked, his eyes wide and incredulous.

"Those", said Albert, "were humans."

"Peeew!" said Samantha. "They smelled bad."

"Everything connected to humans seems to be terribly loud and smell bad" said Emily. "They are the only creatures who do not completely follow the laws of nature. It is best to stay far away from them. Their lives are often troubled and unstable, and they lack serenity."

"When we return south on the migration, you will see more of them. They like to fly but they have no wings, so they ride inside those loud, smelly things. I've never been this close to one before" said Albert. "We used to be able to escape them by coming north to the nesting grounds, but I see that they have come here too. You will see much more of humans later as we go south in the migration. Many of them live in great colonies which stretch farther than you can see but we do our best to avoid them whenever possible."

As the excitement of the day began to wind down, the swan family returned to their simple life. As August turned into September, the cygnets awoke one morning to a light dusting of snow upon the ground. The weather was becoming distinctly colder and most mornings they could see their breath condense in the frosty air. Nighttime darkness also began to return, at first only a few minutes but each night a bit more. By the end of the first week of September, Albert and Emily looked at the cygnets carefully, then had a quiet discussion between themselves. Afterward, Albert gathered the chicks together and made an announcement.

"Kids, your mom and I both think that it's time you prepared for flying lessons. You're almost fully fledged now but before you learn to fly, you'll need to build up your flight muscles and overall strength. From now on, each day's activities will include exercises. As your wings get stronger, we'll teach you the basics of flight."

"Flying! Alright!" said Sam. And with that, the flight lessons were added to the Cygnets daily routine in Swan school.

"The first thing to know" said Albert, "is that everything in the world that flies takes off and lands into the wind. Wind is very important. Make it a part of your automatic awareness in life, something you know about without thinking." Three young heads nodded in agreed understanding.

"Now, follow me out on the tundra."

The little family left the pond and nest area and walked out on the flat, green open tundra. Albert and Emily scanned the sky and open terrain for dangers and, finding none, turned their attention back to the day's lesson.

"First, line up next to each other, wingtip to wingtip and face into the wind."

With a bit of shuffling about, the three cygnets managed to form themselves into a reasonably straight line.

"Now, spread out just a bit more so you don't wack each other with your wings" said Albert, remembering his own flight training many years before. "Now-lift and spread your wings, as far as you can and hold them there." After about a minute, Albert could see that the chicks wings were beginning to droop just a bit, so he told them to lower their wings, then flap them a time or two. He and Emily demonstrated the proper technique for the chicks.

"OK—now each day I want you to do this exercise many times, all throughout the day. It will strengthen your flight muscles. When your muscles are strong enough, I'll show you how to take off and land."

Over the next few days, the chicks competed with each other to see who could flap their wings the hardest and longest. It was fun and each day their wing muscles grew stronger and stronger. A few days later, a cold wind was blowing out of the north. Albert and Emily decided it was the perfect day for the chicks to make their first flight.

"OK, chicks, today's the day!" said Albert. "Perfect conditions for your first

flight. Get in a line, one behind the other."

"Me first" said Sam, running to the front. Cynthia and Samantha rushed right behind him.

"Leave about two feet between you and the bird in front of you" said Albert. "You don't want to crash into each other. Now, watch me and I'll demonstrate the proper technique. Face into the wind and stretch your neck forward. At the same time, start running, unfold your wings and begin flapping. Like this...." And on his third step, Albert's great wings suddenly lifted him gracefully into the air. Then he slowed and reversed the procedure and settled back onto the tundra.

"See—there's nothing to it. Are you ready to try a short hop?"

"Yes! Yes! Yes!" the three chicks shouted with excitement, jumping excitedly from one foot to the other. "Let's go!"

"OK—Lean into the wind, neck straight ahead, start running, begin flapping, 1, 2, 3..." The cold, steady north wind was a big help. On the third step, young wings flapping like mad, the cygnets rose into the air.

"Hey mom! Look at me! I'm flying, I'm flying!" Sam shouted excitedly.

"You certainly are" Emily replied with encouragement. "Good job!"

The cygnets never rose more than a foot or two into the air and they didn't go very far before they began to tire. As soon as their wings slowed down, they fell out of the air quickly as the tundra rose up to meet them. They tumbled and cartwheeled into three piles of feathers, popped to their feet and shouted "Let's go again! *Again!*"

Albert and Emily glided to a landing beside the chicks, listening to their excited calls for more flights.

"It seems that in all the excitement, I forgot to tell you about landing" laughed Albert. "Flights aren't supposed to end in crash landings. You don't want to damage your wings or feathers, so watch while I demonstrate how it's done."

With that, Albert took off, gained a little altitude and swung behind the cygnets, approaching them from the rear.

"Pay close attention to your father" said Emily. "See how he's beginning to pull back as he approaches the ground. That's to dissipate his airspeed, to stop his forward movement. Then, as he's about to contact the ground, he leans even further back and begins to move his legs so that when he touches the ground, they will absorb the remainder of his forward speed." With that, Albert made two short steps and stopped gently.

The chicks were quick learners and after a few more short flights, they were doing well. Not perfect but very good for a first day of practice. The cygnets loved flying (almost all birds do) and the more they practiced, the better they became. When they were reasonably skilled at taking off and landing from the tundra, Albert and Emily showed them how to do it from the water. Takeoffs were about the same, but landings were a bit different. Instead of running a step or two to cushion the landing, the young birds learned to bleed off their airspeed just before impact with the surface so that they ended the flight with a soft settling on the water's surface.

For the next several days, the young birds practiced their flying and became better and better. Their flight muscles grew stronger and stronger. Toward the end of September, at the end of the day, they held a family council.

"Your mom and I are really pleased with the way you're flying has progressed. We think you'll do just fine when the great migration begins." Said Albert.

"What's the great migration?" asked Samantha.

"Well, maybe you've noticed that the days are getting shorter and shorter and the nights are becoming longer and longer. Also, the temperature is getting colder and colder each day. Some mornings there is even a thin skin of ice on the ponds. The food is also beginning to disappear."

"Yeah" said Sam. "There's not as much to eat and the juicy water bugs have almost disappeared."

"That is because winter is coming. Before it fully arrives, we need to be gone, headed south. That is what the great migration is all about." Said Emily. "Winter and dark and very, very cold. All green things die, and our food disappears. We cannot live here in winter, so we fly south to warmer climates. That time has almost come."

"How do we know when to start" asked Cynthia?

"You will hear the Flight Call" said Emily. "Listen carefully and I will sing it for you." With that, Emily raised her head and from deep within her came a beautiful, resonant sound—"ou, ou, ou". Albert joined in with a sound like "oh, oh, oh". "Oh, how beautiful!" said Cynthia.

"Isn't that like the Forward Call you taught us?" said Sam.

"It's very similar but shorter in duration. Listen carefully. Here's the flight call again. Ou, ou, ou. Now the Forward Call: Oo, oo, oo. Do you hear the difference?

"Oh, yeah I've got it now" said Sam as the three young birds practiced the calls. Their voices were higher pitched than their parents, but they quickly mastered the slight differences between the two calls.

"In the evening, just before dusk, when you hear all of the swans singing the Flight Call, you know that the time has come to begin the migration." Said Emily.

The next morning dawned cold and clear with a heavy frost covering the ground. After a quick breakfast, the family made a short flight to view things from the air. It was nearly the end of September and the tundra which had been like a carpet of green all summer now appeared as a beautiful medley of colors as the vegetation slowly died and changed into the reds, yellows and countless varieties of vibrant shades which marked the start of Autumn.

"How lovely it all looks" said Samantha. "It's gorgeous."

"And look at all of the swans!" said Cynthia. I have never seen so many gathered in one place before."

"It's an exciting time of year" said Emily. Many of these are friends and family that we haven't seen since we arrived four months ago. Let's stop and visit." She led the family to a large lake that seemed to be covered in swans and cygnets. They landed and joined with the multitude of other swans who were already crowded together. There was an excitement in the air that everyone felt. The cygnets quickly met other first year cygnets and blended in with their group. Albert and Emily met a couple who had flown north in their flock earlier that Spring. Everywhere they looked there were happy, excited swans.

Albert had joined a group of other cobs, all discussing some aspect of the migration. "The food's about gone here. We need to get on our way."

"Yes" added Albert, "We don't want to get caught in an early winter. That could be bad for everyone."

"Quite right" added another cob. "The kids are so excited it's hard to hold them back. Heck, I'm excited too. Summer's over and it's time to head south." All the other cobs murmured in agreement.

"I saw a ptarmigan the other day and its feathers were almost pure white-a sure sign that winter's almost upon us." Said another cob.

"Same thing with the arctic foxes." Said another. "I saw one from the air yesterday and its coat was almost pure white. The snow can't be far off." Everyone could feel that something big was about to occur.

Albert, Emily and the cygnets spent that night with their friends on the big lake. There was no point in going back to their pond. The food was almost all gone and besides, they all felt the urge to mingle with other swans. That evening, in the hour just before sunset as they were completing the final preening of the day, Sam said "Hey-listen!" The family stopped their preening and focused on the sounds around them.

"I can hear it!" said Samantha. "Mom! It's the flight call!" And indeed, it was. At first, only a few swans were singing but more and more joined in until the darkness of night caused a silence across the tundra.

The following morning, there was considerable excitement in the swan world. There was much nervous swimming to and fro and visiting in small groups. Albert and Emily gathered their family together and told them that the migration would probably begin within one or two days but there was one last thing which they needed to know.

"You need to learn some things about formation flying" said Albert. "Come take a flight with your mom and me so we can show you what you need to know."

The family became airborne and Albert and Emily demonstrated how to fly in a "V" formation.

"This is done by positioning yourself about 45 degrees either left or right of the swan in front of you and slightly higher. That way you avoid the turbulence created by the birds before you and have relatively clear, calm air to fly in. It allows you to fly more efficiently and use less energy."

Albert led the way and Emily demonstrated how to position properly both to the left, then to the right. The young swans caught on quickly and were soon flying in their own little family "V" of five. Once the technique was mastered, the family returned to a small lake dotted with swans. Cynthia had a question.

"When the migration begins, do we all take off together and fly in a giant "V"?

"Oh, no—that would be too awkward and clumsy and take too much time" said Emily. "We'll take off and form up in family groups of 85 or a hundred, maybe less. Each group will then form itself into several "V's". Oh, look—there goes a group now."

The family looked up and saw a flock of about 30 swans formed into 4 loose "V's". gliding gracefully through the air.

"Is it time to go?" Samantha asked with excited anticipation.

"Almost, but not quite yet" said Emily. "If we all left at the same time, there would be too many of us and we would overwhelm the rest areas and the food supply. Listen for the flight song. When everyone in our area sings it, we know it's time to go."

"I hope it's soon" said Sam. "There's hardly any food here left to eat."

"Well, that brings up another thing you should know" said Emily. "Not every place we stop will have the food we're familiar with. Some areas won't even have much water, just big flat fields of grain. You've never had grain before but just stick close and we'll show you what to do." The chicks nodded in understanding and then swam off with some other first year cygnets to look for food. Later that evening, the little family was preening just before dusk. When they had finished, Emily raised her head and began the flight call. It floated out on the still night air, a melodic song full of memories from years past. Albert joined in and for a while the two voices were the only sound floating over the vast tundra. Then the cygnets began the call, their voices higher pitched than their parents but blending nicely. As the last rays of daylight began to fade, first one, then another swan began to join in until the night air became alive with the musical murmurings of thousands upon thousands of swans. The call went out and enveloped the land like a warm blanket of sound, bonding the swans in a united effort. All sang the ancient, beautiful melody, joining their hearts in a common time and purpose. When the song finally ceased, Emily said quietly, with great authority: "Tomorrow is the day. We will leave in the morning."

The first faint glimmer of light began to reach the roosting swans while three young pairs of eyes popped fully open.

"I can see light" said Sam excitedly. "Time to go!"

"Mom, is it time yet?" asked Cynthia, looking up at her sleepy parents.

"Oh, I'm so excited" said Samantha. "Our first migration! Hooray!"

"OK, just settle down" said Albert, knowing that there was still plenty of time to begin the day and wishing that he had been able to have a few more minutes of sleep. "There are still a few things to do before we leave here. First off is food. Never pass up a chance to eat. It takes a lot of energy to fly for two months."

"After that, we preen really well." Said Emily. "We want to begin with our feathers in tip top shape."

"I'm too excited to eat." Said Sam, the first time any of them had ever heard him make that statement.

"Nevertheless, you need to eat something. We don't want you running out of energy halfway through the morning." Replied Emily, though she knew that his plump little body had plenty of fat reserves to see him safely through the migration.

As the cygnets rushed off to grab some last-minute bugs or some lingering green forage, Albert and Emily slowly stretched their wings and looked around quietly for a bit of breakfast. To be honest, there wasn't much. That summer's bugs were mostly gone or burrowed deeply into the mud. The green forage that had been so plentiful all summer was also gone. Weeks of frosty mornings and diminishing sunlight had all but wiped it out. Only under water could a bit of lingering vegetation still be found. Indeed, it was time to leave this place.

After a hurried breakfast, the birds completed a full and careful preening under Emily's expert supervision. At length, the three cygnets stood before their parents, eagerly hopping from one foot to the other.

"Is it time? Is it time?" they kept asking.

In answer, Emily and Albert raised their heads and began the ancient melody of the Flight Call. As it flowed out over the tundra, it was picked up by the other swans and repeated, swelling in volume until the entire land vibrated with the murmuring harmony of thousands of voices. This song triggered within the swans all the pent-up emotion and longing that had been held back over the past days. Now they were united. Now they were ready. It was time to start.

"OK, guys-follow me." Said Albert. He took two quick steps, spread his great wings and lifted smoothly into the air. Sam followed quickly, remembering to take up position to the left. Samantha took her position to the right, Cynthia to the left of Sam and finally Emily in the trailing position to the right so she could see the whole family. Everywhere they looked, they could see swans taking to the air and forming the great migratory flight "V's". Another great cycle had ended and a new one begun and that was just the way that nature intended it to be.

Definitions

Beaufort Sea: A geographic area adjacent to the Arctic Ocean, and the north slope of Alaska.

Cob: male swan

Pen: female swan

Wintering ground: A geographic area where swans spend the winter.

Tundra swans (formerly called Whistling Swans): They have a distinctive yellow and black bill markings that differentiate them from other swans.

Preening: Grooming done by all waterbirds to water proof their feathers.

Spit of land: A narrow area of land surrounded by water on three sides

Bills: The area around the mouth that looked like small jagged teeth, used to catch and eat aquatic plants and algae.

Fledgling: is a young bird that has grown enough to acquire its initial flight feathers and is preparing to leave the nest and care for itself.

Jaegers: A bird that preys and feeds upon other birds.

Cygnets: A young immature swan.

Cygnus columbianus: Commonly called tundra swan, (formerly known as whistling swans).

North Slope: An area approximately a hundred miles wide, stretching from the Brooks Range to the arctic ocean.

Printed in the United States
By Bookmasters